The Little Island

For the ducks, the geese and ALL the animals on the little island that I call home.
And for Ben – who lets nothing ruffle his fine feathers, and whose
quackers idea this was in the first place. With love – S.P-H.

To anyone I've ever met who came from somewhere else;
my life is richer because of you. – R.S.

"No goose is an island entire of itself; every goose
is a piece of the continent, a part of the main..."
– John Duck (1624)

First published in Great Britain in 2019 by Andersen Press Ltd., 20 Vauxhall Bridge Road, London SW1V 2SA.
Text copyright © Smriti Prasadam-Halls 2019. Illustration copyright © Robert Starling 2019.
The rights of Smriti Prasadam-Halls and Robert Starling to be identified
as the author and illustrator of this work have been asserted by them in
accordance with the Copyright, Designs and Patents Act, 1988.
All rights reserved. Printed and bound in China.
1 3 5 7 9 10 8 6 4 2
British Library Cataloguing in Publication Data available.
ISBN 978 1 78344 909 5

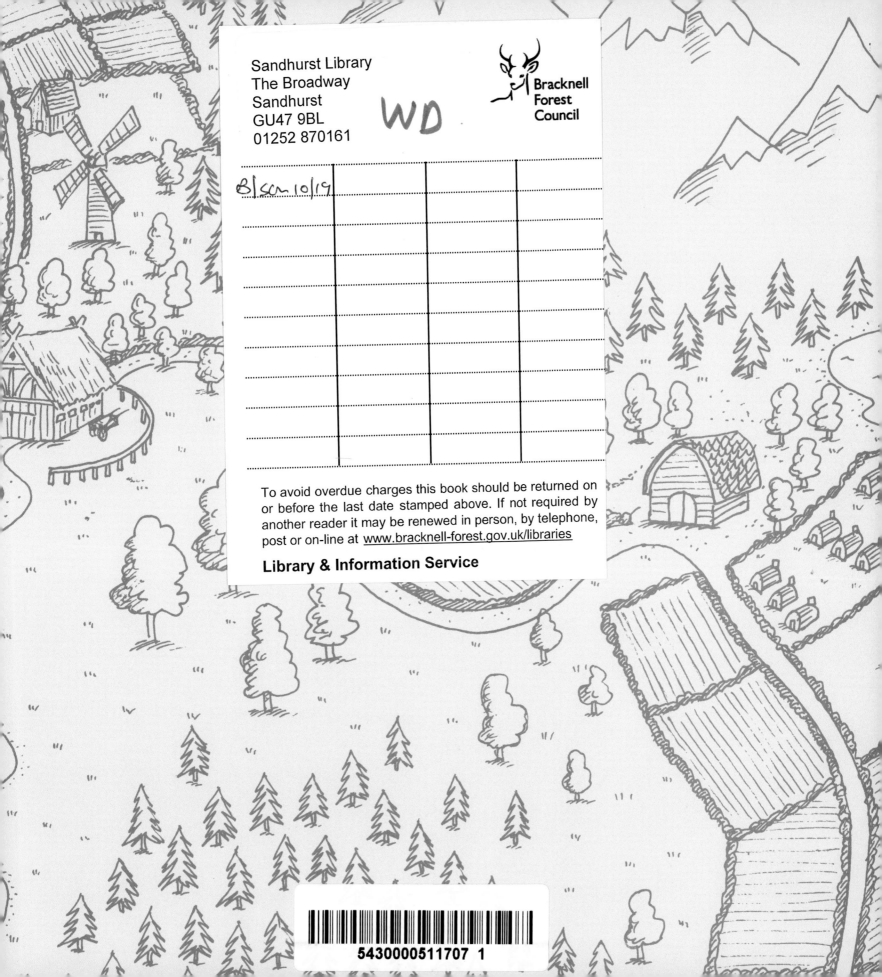

The Little Island

Smriti Prasadam-Halls   Robert Starling

ANDERSEN PRESS

There was once a farm where all the animals were friends. They worked hard and each was at liberty to live and work where they chose.
Together they looked after the farm and each other.

It wasn't perfect and they didn't always agree
(animals almost never do). But they liked it.

The ducks and geese lived on a pond at the edge of the farm.

They waddled about on a little island of soft, sunny slopes, lush green reeds and golden fruit trees.

One day, the geese began to gossip. Soon they were in a flap.

"Why do the other animals come to our part of the farm so often?" honked one.

"There really isn't room for everyone here!" honked another.

"No one listens to us!"

"We aren't safe!"

They groused and they grumbled late into the night.

That night the geese called a meeting.

"Our island was once a green and pleasant land!" they declared to the ducks. "The apples were much redder. The grass was much greener. The sun was much warmer. And the food tasted better!

Now it's too busy. We should leave the rest of the farm and live on our own, just as we please."

The ducks thought this was a dreadful idea. They loved living and working together with the other animals. But there were more geese than ducks...

And so the geese peck-peck-pecked away until there was no longer a footbridge to the island.

The animals on the rest of the farm looked on sadly.
Then they shook their heads, bid farewell to their
dear old friends and went back to work.

At first, nothing much changed.
The sun shone, the bees
buzzed and life was good.

But very soon the ducks and geese found
they had to work harder. Much harder.
There were so many jobs to do now.

Mending...
fixing...
building...

Cleaning...
chopping...
cooking...

The geese had not noticed how helpful the other animals had been (animals almost never do).

Summer came and the grass grew tall and green,
just as the geese remembered…

but without the sheep and cows grazing, it soon
scorched and withered in the sun.

"We mustn't complain!" grumbled the geese, tails drooping.
"At least we are happy."

Autumn came and the fruit trees were full...

but without the help of the horses and goats
to gather the harvest, the geese went hungry.

"We mustn't complain!" grumbled the geese, tummies rumbling.
"At least we are happy."

Winter came and the animals on the farm
huddled together cosily to keep warm.

But without their old friends, the geese were cold.
"We m-m-mustn't c-c-complain!" grumbled the
geese, beaks chattering. "At least we are happy."

The next year was hard, the following
year was harder, and the year after that...

... the foxes came.

The foxes looked slyly at the little island.
No roosters to raise the alarm.
No pigs to make trouble.
No cows to chase them away.
DINNER TIME!

It was perfect, the foxes agreed
(which animals almost never do).
They liked it.

At dead of night, silently, speedily,
they surveyed the island.

Silently, stealthily, they slunk into the water.
Silently, swiftly, they swam across the pond.

Silently, sneakily, they stole on to land.
Silently, soundlessly... (yes, you get the picture).

Feet flapped and feathers flew.

"Help! Help!" shrieked the geese and the ducks in terror. "SAVE US!"

The animals on the farm rushed to the water's edge.
But alas... there was no footbridge to reach the island.

And so the farm animals did something
that animals almost never do...

They BELLOWED and YELLED

ALL NIGHT LONG...

until the foxes, who as we know prefer to
work in silence, slid away into the night.

AA!
CLANG!
BLEA
CLANG!
AT!
NEEEIII GGGHH!
HEE-HAW!!
CLANG!
O!
MOOOOOHH!
MOO!
HEE HAW
OINK!
MOO!
CLANG!
OINK!
BAAA!
BAAA!
K! OINK!
OINK!
OINK!

In the morning, the ducks and the geese wanted to thank their old friends. They remembered how once they had all lived and worked together.

It hadn't been perfect and they hadn't always agreed (animals almost never do). But they had liked it.

Their green and pleasant
island was in ruins.
The barn was broken
and the crops
were trampled.

There was so much to do and they did not know where to start.
And then they had an idea...

Carefully, they collected long pieces of wood... and nails... and screws...

And then slowly, very slowly...

they began to build a bridge.

All the way back to the farm.

The End